The Gallery Cat

For Elizabeth and Zoë — S. B.

For Saffy, the studio cat — T. R.

To coincide with its reopening in 2002, Manchester Art Gallery invited the acclaimed
children's author and illustrator Tony Ross to respond to twenty-four works in the collection.
He produced a series of drawings which make a witty visual comment on the originals.
These illustrations have been the inspiration and impetus for *The Gallery Cat*.

For information about Manchester Art Gallery, please visit
www.manchestergalleries.org.uk

Text copyright © 2004 by Stella Blackstone
Illustrations copyright © 2004 by Tony Ross
The moral right of Stella Blackstone to be identified as the author and
Tony Ross to be identified as the illustrator of this work has been asserted

All photographs of the original artworks are © Manchester City Galleries
Manchester City Galleries own the copyright of works, or have made every effort
to secure permission from copyright holders

Tony Ross illustrations purchased with the help of the Heritage Lottery Fund

This publication is being made possible with the help of Manchester City Galleries Development Trust

First published in Great Britain in 2004 by Barefoot Books Ltd, 124 Walcot St, Bath BA1 5BG
All rights reserved. No part of this book may be reproduced in any form or by any means,
electronic or mechanical, including photocopying, recording or by any information storage
and retrieval system, without permission in writing from the publisher

Graphic design by Tracey Woodward
Colour separation by Grafiscan, Verona
Printed and bound in China

This book has been printed on 100% acid-free paper

ISBN 1-901223-39-6

British Cataloguing-in-Publication Data: a catalogue record
for this book is available from the British Library

1 3 5 7 9 8 6 4 2

Front cover art incorporates:
Oxford Road, Manchester 1910 Adolphe Valette

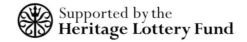 Supported by the
Heritage Lottery Fund

 MANCHESTER
CITY COUNCIL

Manchester Art Gallery

The Gallery Cat

Stella **Blackstone** and *Tony* **Ross**

Barefoot Books
Celebrating Art and Story

It was only the first week of the holidays, and as usual, it was raining. Adam and Katy were bored.

'Why don't you go to the art gallery?' suggested Valette, the family cat. 'They're running a painting class later this morning.'

'The art gallery? Oh, please no,' said Katy. 'I never know what to look at in pictures.'

'Neither do I.' Adam sank into his chair. 'Art galleries are dull, dull, dull. Can't you think of anything better for us to do, Valette?'

'It might be more fun than you think.' said Valette. 'I was there only last night, and I saw lots of fascinating things. Bring along your sketchpads and you might be pleasantly surprised.'

'All right,' said Adam. 'But you'll have to make yourself invisible, otherwise we'll get into trouble — cats aren't allowed in art galleries during the day.'

'Don't worry,' Valette retorted. 'I know how to look after myself.'

So off they went.

Old Cab at All Saints
1911   Adolphe Valette

Valette had to make himself invisible straight away to get past the entrance. He hid under Katy's coat and nudged her legs to steer them into the galleries.

'I wonder what instruments those women are playing,' said Katy. 'They don't look very cheerful, do they?'

'What they need is a bit of pop music,' said Adam. 'That would liven them up.' And he drew a sketch of two girls dancing together in a meadow.

The Bower Meadow
1850–1872 Dante Gabriel Rossetti

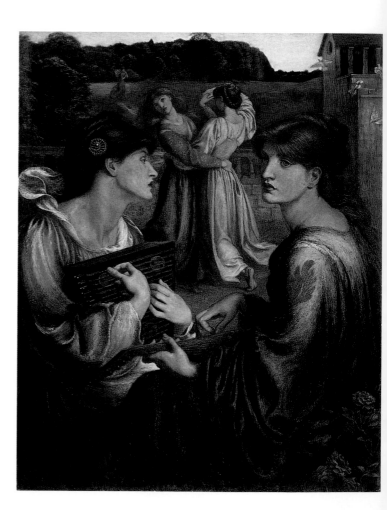

Valette poked his head out.

'Come this way!' he said.

'She's gathering firewood, isn't she?' said Katy.
And she remembered how Adam always messed
about when they stayed at their Gran's cottage,
and went out to gather sticks for the fire. He
thought it was much more fun climbing trees.

A Peasant Girl Gathering Faggots in a Wood
1782   Thomas Gainsborough

Valette heard a party of visitors approaching and gave Katy a nudge.

'Time to move on — it's getting too crowded in here.' He trotted off to another gallery and the children hurried after him.

'Who's that?' asked Adam, peering at the caption of a big oil painting. 'It says "Manfred on the Jungfrau".'

'A troubled hero, I expect,' said Valette. 'Some of you humans get so worked-up about life. You could learn a trick or two from us cats, you know.'

'Is the man coming up behind going to rescue him?' asked Katy.

'He's going to be swallowed up by the mountain,' declared Valette.

That gave Adam another idea…

Manfred on the Jungfrau 1840–1861 Ford Madox Brown

'What are you doing?' Adam had finished his sketch, and he stood behind Katy, screwing up his face.

'I'm doing "Portrait of an Unfortunate Girl",' said Katy. 'She's trying to pull out her own tooth so that she doesn't have to go to the dentist, like the man in that painting over there.'

'Yuk,' said Adam.

The Dentist
1652   David Teniers

'Do we have to look at everything?' Katy asked Valette.

'Certainly not! Just choose what you like the look of, and see what happens.'

'What do you look at when you come here?'

'Well, for a start, being a creature of the night, I am verrry attracted to this moonlit castle. Have either of you ever looked at the kind of shadows that the moon makes?'

Adam thought for a bit. He couldn't remember seeing moon shadows, but he knew about the kind of shadow a candle makes, so he tried drawing that.

Caernarvon Castle by Moonlight
1780–1785 (circa) Joseph Wright of Derby

14

'I'll show you something you might enjoy,' said Valette, and he steered
Katy to another gallery where there was a picture that was full of umbrellas.

'Imagine someone holding an umbrella.'

'Right…'

'Now imagine the sun is shining outside the umbrella.'

'Right…'

'Now imagine it's raining inside the umbrella.'

'You're mad,' said Katy.

'Wrong. I am simply a cat with a creative mind,' said Valette.

Umbrellas
1917 Dorothy Brett

Adam wandered about until he came to a huge seascape. There was a big sailing boat in the middle of the painting, with a member of the crew throwing a long rope over to people beside it, who were in a rowing boat.

Valette stalked up and stood beside him. He coughed nervously.

'Erghh,' he shivered. 'Cats and water do not go together. Nothing would induce me to go to sea.'

Katy agreed. 'I'll draw a boat, but not one as big as that,' she said. 'And it doesn't have to be on water. I'll give it a rope, too, to pull it along.'

'In nautical terms,' Valette remarked coolly, 'that is not called a rope — it's a painter. So you see, the title of the painting is a sort of joke.'

Now for the Painter (Rope) — Passengers Going on Board
1827   J.M.W. Turner

In the next gallery, there was a picture of a baby drifting along a river in a cradle.

'Look, Valette!' said Katy. 'There's a cat on the cradle, too!'

'Don't let that give you any ideas,' said Valette. 'I've already told you that cats and water don't go together.'

But Adam had overheard him. He flipped open his sketchpad, and before you could say 'Wet Cat!' Valette was adrift.

'…otherwise you might drown,' Adam explained.

'Hmph,' Valette retorted, when he saw Adam's drawing.

A Flood
1870 Sir John Millais

'Don't take any notice of him, Valette,' said Katy. 'I've seen something much more enjoyable for you. Look at this — "Ship Inn, Mousehole".'

'Ah yes,' said Valette. 'There is something particularly inspiring about this scene. Makes me long for a tasty morsel of mouse, and perhaps an appetising fillet of goldfish for good measure…'

Ship Inn, Mousehole
1930   Christopher Wood

'Have a look at this,' said Adam. 'It's amazing. It's called the Prometheus Vase.'

'Pro — what?' asked Katy.

'Pro-metheus,' Adam repeated grandly. 'I've learnt about him in school. He was a Greek hero who stole fire from the gods, and they punished him by tying him to a rock.'

'How very uncomfortable,' remarked Valette. 'Never play with fire, in my opinion. Much too easy to get burnt — look what's happened to him. Ouch!'

'Valette, shhh!' hissed Katy.

Prometheus Vase
Made by Minton 1875–1878
Probably designed by Victor Simyan

But Valette was getting into his stride.

'Have you learnt about Jason and the Argonauts yet?'

'I think we're doing that next term.'

'Well, when the Argonauts ran out of drinking water, Jason sent Hylas to collect some fresh supplies from a deserted island — but it wasn't deserted after all.'

'Pesky girls,' said Adam. 'They're always spying on boys like that, trying to interfere and get all the attention.'

'We'd better move on,' said Katy. 'Adam won't stop talking.'

Hylas and the Nymphs
1896
John William Waterhouse

'You've got ten more minutes,' said Valette. 'Then the painting class starts.'

'I just want to do one more picture!' said Katy.

Adam and Valette watched.

'Too romantic for me,' said Adam. 'All those hearts everywhere. The football's the only interesting part, but you've painted it the wrong shape.'

'I'm being symbolic,' Katy retorted.

'Verrry good,' murmured Valette.

Early Lovers 1858 Frederick Smallfield

The children followed Valette to the studio where the painting class was being held.

'Let's take it in turns to paint each other,' said Katy.

'Okay, toss a coin to see who's first.'

Katy won.

Adam stood on a cube holding a football and tried to look heroic. 'I think you'd be more comfortable sitting down,' Valette suggested. Then he whispered to Katy, 'I'd paint him red if I were you.'

'Would you?' asked Katy. 'Why?'

'Because you don't always have to paint exactly what you see when you paint a portrait,' said Valette. 'And I happen to like red.'

Katy dipped her paintbrush into the red pot.

'Why have you chosen that?' asked Adam, looking at her sideways.

'PLEASE sit still and concentrate,' said Katy. 'You're supposed to be posing, not talking.'

So Adam sat still, and Katy painted, and Valette, who was rather enjoying his day as the gallery cat, stretched himself out and purred.

Sir Gregory Page-Turner
1768 Pompeo Batoni

A Footnote about Valette

You may be wondering where Valette lives and how much time he spends at the art gallery. We couldn't find out much about him because he doesn't enjoy giving interviews, and he prefers to visit the gallery by night, when there are no people around. However, we do know that he takes his name from the French artist, Adolphe Valette, who lived in Manchester from 1905 to 1928. The picture below is a self-portrait of Valette the artist. You can find several other paintings by Valette the artist at Manchester Art Gallery. If you look carefully, you may see a glimpse of Valette the cat, too — and if you listen, you may even hear him giving his very particular opinion on some of the masterpieces there.

Self-Portrait   1917 (circa)   Adolphe Valette